Little Bunny's Bathtime!

Jane Johnson

illustrated by

Gaby Hansen

Little Tiger Press

London

"Bathtime for my bunnies!"
called Mrs Rabbit, and her
children all came running.
All except her youngest
little bunny.

"I don't want a bath,"
said Little Bunny.
"I want to go on playing."

"You really want to play all by
yourself?" asked his mummy.
Little Bunny nodded, but
now he wasn't so sure.

"Well, you be good while
I'm busy with the others,"
said Mrs Rabbit, plopping
them into the water.

"Swish, swash, swoosh," sang
the little rabbits happily, swirling
their bubbles into a heap.

   Little Bunny wanted
to play too.

"Look at me!" he called,
hiding behind the towels.

"Yes, dear," said Mrs Rabbit, but
she went on washing the others.
"Tickly, wickly, wiggle toes," giggled
her little bunnies, waggling their
feet in the water.

"Guess where I am!"
shouted Little Bunny,
hidden in the linen
basket.

"Found you," smiled his
mother, lifting the lid . . .

But she turned back
to finish washing
the others.

"Up you come!" puffed Mrs Rabbit,
lifting her children out of the tub.

"Rub-a-dub-dub, you've all had a scrub!"
she laughed. "What lovely clean
bunnies you are!"

Little Bunny was cross.
He wanted his mummy
to notice *him*.

So he
climbed
up . . .

and up − as far
as he could.
But suddenly . . .

. . . SPLOSH!

He fell into the bath!

"Oh my!" said Mrs Rabbit, fishing
him out straight away.
Little Bunny gazed up at her happily.
"I'm ready for a bath now, Mummy,"
he said, smiling sweetly.

Mrs Rabbit couldn't
help smiling back.
 "Off you go and play
quietly," she said to
the others.

Then she ran
fresh water and gave
Little Bunny a bath –
all to himself.

"Soapy ears and soapy toes,
soapy little bunny nose!" sang Mrs Rabbit.
She washed his ears while he fluffed
up some new bubbles.
"I love you, Mummy," said Little Bunny.
"I love you too, darling."

She washed his back while
he played with his boat.
 "You're my best mummy in the
whole world," said Little Bunny.
 "And you're my precious
bunnykin."

She dried his fur
and whiskers, and said,
"Ooh, you smell
so clean and nice!"

And Little Bunny kissed his mummy
and hugged her tight.

"There now, all done," sighed Mrs Rabbit.
"It's time for bed. Where are my other
little bunnies?"

She found them in the kitchen.
"Oh no! What a mess!" cried
Mrs Rabbit. "You're dirty again!
You all need *another* bath!"

"Yes," giggled Little Bunny.
"All except me!"